Marlene

Disney

ENCHANTED TALES

This Edition Exclusive to:

INNOVAGE

(949) 587-9207

Produced and published by
INNOVAGE, INC.
19511 Pauling
Foothill Ranch, California,
92610
Tel: (949) 587-9207
Fax: (949) 587-9024

Printed in CHINA

CONTENTS

101 Dalmatians
2

Beauty and the Beast
44

Jungle Book
80

Lion King
112

Little Mermaid
144

Peter Pan
180

Pocahontas
218

Sleeping Beauty
254

Disney's 101 DALMATIANS

Hi! My name is Pongo. This story began one beautiful spring day. Roger, my pet, was busy trying to write a song. He's a musician and practically married to his work.

I thought life would be more interesting if we had a companion. So I was looking out the window for a suitable mate. Two really, one for Roger, and one for me.

That's when I saw her, a beautiful Dalmatian. Her human looked nice, too. "Perfect!" I decided.

It took some quick thinking to get Roger away from his work. But soon I was able to convince him to go for a walk.

I spotted them as soon as we entered the park. The Dalmatian was named Perdita. She was wonderful!

But as usual, Roger had his head in the clouds. He barely noticed Perdita's human, Anita. Sometimes I wonder about these human beings.

Finally, I wound my leash around their legs, and tipped them into the pond. That got them to notice each other, all right! It also got Perdita to notice me.

Well, before long, Roger asked Anita to marry him, and Perdita agreed to marry me, too. It was a beautiful double wedding.

After that, our house became a paradise for dogs and their humans. We were even happier when we discovered that Perdita was expecting puppies.

When the big day came and I saw those fifteen little white balls of fluff, I was the proudest father on the block!

Unfortunately Cruella De Vil had to burst in and shatter our peace.

I heard that Perdita and Pongo have fifteen puppies," Cruella said, pulling out a checkbook and pen. "How much do you want for all of them?"

Anita tried to be polite. After all, she had known Cruella in school. But no matter how much money Cruella offered, Roger was firm. "The puppies are not for sale!" he said.

Cruella was so angry that she stormed out of the house, shouting threats. I had the feeling she meant trouble.

Over the next few weeks, the puppies grew quickly. They were such fun!

They loved to watch television. Their hero was a dog called Thunderbolt. Sometimes, they barked and growled when the bad guys appeared on the screen.

One evening, Perdita and I went out for a stroll with Roger and Anita. We left the puppies at home with Nanny. She was the one who looked after all of us.

Nanny had just put the puppies to bed when the doorbell rang. There stood two shady-looking men who said they worked for the electric company. Nanny was suspicious, and wouldn't let them in. But they pushed their way past her.

"**W**here do you think you're going?" she cried.

Nanny tried her best, but she couldn't stop them.
Soon they found the what they were after. They found
the puppies.

When we got home, the puppies' basket was empty.

Roger called the police right way. "Our fifteen Dalmatian puppies have been stolen," he told them. "I don't know who could have done this. But please, you must find them for us."

Perdita and I were not about to wait for the police to solve the kidnapping. We decided to take matters into our own hands.

The next evening, I used the Twilight Bark to send out word of the kidnapping. What a racket! I'm sure no one in the city got much sleep that night.

But it worked. The dogs in the city were the first to hear the news. They barked the message to Towser the bloodhound and Lucy the goose, who lived out in the country.

"What is it? What's all the gossip?" asked Lucy.

"Fifteen puppies stolen!" answered Towser. "We'd best send the word along. It will be up to me to reach the Colonel!"

Then Towser began to bark with all his might, passing the message on to the Colonel, an old English sheepdog.

The Colonel and his friend Sergeant Tibs the cat set to work immediately.

I just remembered," Tibs told the Colonel. "Two nights past, I heard puppies barking at the old De Vil mansion."

"That place has been empty for years. Something fishy is going on over there," the Colonel said. "Let's go have a look."

Sure enough, there were signs of activity at the old mansion, so the Colonel sent Tibs to get a closer look.

What a scene! Two tough-looking men named Horace and Jasper were watching televsion. And all around them were spotted puppies!

Tibs snuck closer to one of the puppies.

"Are you one of the fifteen stolen puppies?" Tibs whispered. "There's ninety-nine of us altogether," answered the pup.

Meanwhile, the Colonel had passed on the news that the puppies had been found. Of course, upon learning this, Perdita and I raced to rescue our pups.

Tibs knew there was no time to waste when he overheard Cruella De Vil arrive at the house and begin talking to Horace and Jasper. She was planning to make spotted coats out of the puppies!

"I've got no time to argue!" she shouted. "I want the job on those puppies to be done tonight!"

"We'll get on with it – as soon as the show's over," Jasper said to Horace after Cruella had left.

"Quick!" Tibs whispered to the puppies. "Follow me and don't make a sound! You're in danger. I've got to get you out of here now!"

The puppies were frightened, but they did as they were told.

Tibs led the puppies to a hole in the living room wall. Then, just as he was pushing the last pup through, Horace and Jasper noticed the dogs were missing.

Jasper grabbed a fireplace poker, and Horace picked up a broken chair leg to use as a club. Then they started searching every corner of the old mansion.

Quickly, Tibs hid the puppies under the staircase.

"Shush!" the cat whispered.

But just then, the flashlight's beam lit up their hiding place!

Perdita and I had barely arrived outside the mansion when we heard Horace and Jasper shouting.

"Hurry! Something's going on in there!" I said.

We burst through the window, growling, and quickly went to work saving our puppies.

I latched onto Jasper's leg and soon had him on the floor while Perdita made short work of Horace.

In the meantime, Tibs had managed to get the puppies safely out of the mansion. The Colonel was waiting for them outside and led them to safety at his farm.

Soon Perdita and I were reunited with the puppies. We planned to rest at the Colonel's farm for the night. But when Horace and Jasper showed up, we all had to move on.

The weather was getting much worse, and it was hard for the puppies to walk in the deep snow. Fortunately, we continued to get help from our friends. A Collie who lived on a farm in the area came out to meet us.

" We'd just about lost hope," he said. "We have shelter for you at the dairy farm across the road. You can all rest and get an early start in the morning."

"Thank goodness!" I said.

Three cows watched as Perdita led the puppies into the barn.

"Oh, the poor little dears," said Princess. "They're completely worn out and half frozen."

"Mother, I'm hungry," one of the puppies said.

"Do you like warm milk?" Princess asked.

"Come and get it, kids," said Queenie. "It's on the house!"

The puppies lapped up all the milk they could drink, and then settled down to sleep. But the next day at dawn, we were on the run again.

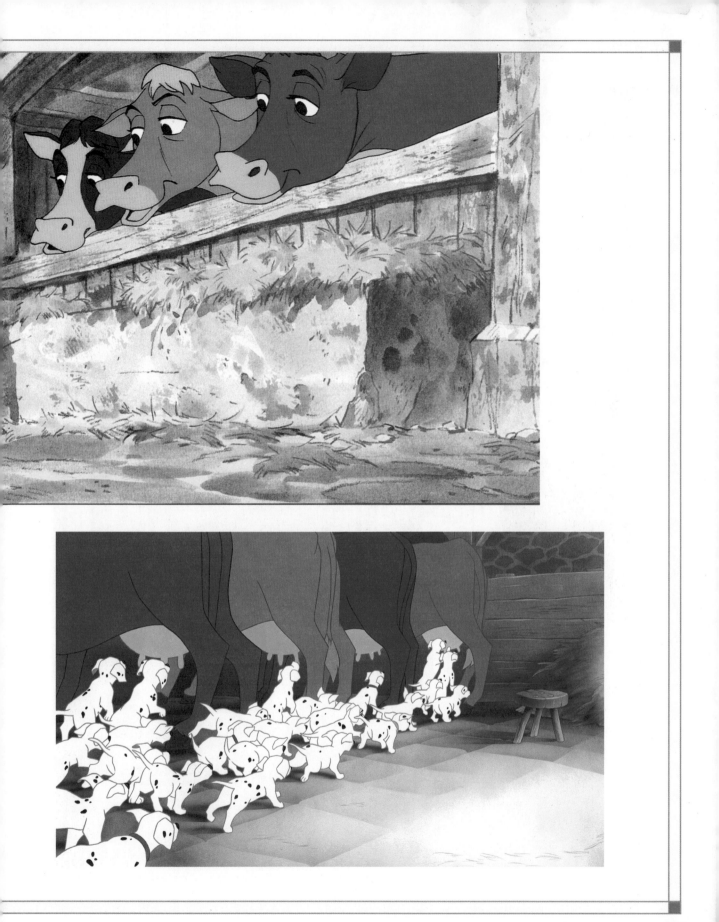

A Labrador Retriever was waiting for us in the next village. He gave us shelter and explained that he had arranged a ride home for us in the back of a van.

Just then, we spotted Cruella De Vil cruising through the village in her car. Nearby, Horace and Jasper were searching for us on foot.

"Oh, Pongo," Perdita said, "how will we get into the van without her seeing us?"

Then I had an idea. "We'll all roll in soot," I said. "She's looking for Dalmatians, not Labradors!"

Soon we were all black from head to tail.

Perdita and the Lab led the first batch of puppies right past Horace and Jasper and into the waiting van.

"Look, Jasper," Horace remarked as the puppies trotted past him. "Do you suppose those dogs have disguised themselves?"

"You idiot!" Jasper laughed. "Dogs don't paint themselves black!"

"Those dogs are somewhere in this village," Cruella yelled to Horace and Jasper. "Now go find them!"

The final batch of puppies had almost made it to the van when...

SPLAAT! Drops of melting snow fell on the puppies. Small white spots began to appear on their backs. Cruella looked more closely. Her brain started ticking. White spots on black dogs...of course!

"After them! After them!" she screamed.

We all made a run for it. Then, just as I lifted the last puppy safely into the van, the engine roared to life, and we were all on our way to London.

"**I**'ll catch up with them, yet!" Cruella said, stepping on the gas pedal. Cruella raced after the van, and rammed into it. She was trying to force us off the road!

We cringed in fear, wishing our driver could go faster. Then I saw the blue truck driven by Horace and Jasper. They had taken a short cut.

 Now they were barreling down the hill, trying to cut off our van. But instead, they smashed into Cruella's car.

BAANNG! CRAASSHH! Cruella, Horace, and Jasper went flying through the air and landed in a pile of snow. They would not be able to cause any more trouble.

A little later, at the house in London, Nanny heard faint barking. The barks got louder. Suddenly the kitchen door burst open, and a pack of black dogs scampered in. One of the big dogs jumped on Anita's lap, and tried to lick her face. "Why, it's Perdy!" Anita cried. "And all the puppies!"

Then she looked again. "There must be a hundred of them!" she said in amazement.

"One hundred and one," said Roger, counting. "Including Perdita and Pongo. What a family!"

Everyone was delighted, even Nanny, who had quite a job on her hands trying to get us all cleaned up.

"What will we do with them all?" asked Anita.

"We'll keep 'em," said Roger. We'll buy a big place in the country and live there. It'll be a plantation. A Dalmatian plantation!"

Roger was so pleased that he sat right down at the piano to write a song.

And we all gathered around him, just happy to be home.

Once upon a time in a faraway land, a young Prince lived in a shining castle. Although he had everything his heart desired, he was selfish and unkind.

One winter's night, an enchantress came to the castle disguised as an old beggar woman. She offered him a single rose in return for shelter from the cold. But the Prince sneered at her gift, and turned her away.

So the enchantress transformed him into a hideous beast, and transformed all his servants into household objects. The spell would be broken only if the Beast could learn to love, and earn someone's love in return before the last petal fell from the enchanted rose.

Ashamed of his ugliness, the Beast locked himself away in his castle. An enchanted mirror was his only window to the outside world.

As the years passed, he lost all hope. For who could ever love a beast?

Not far from the castle, in a small village, lived a beautiful girl named Belle. Belle loved to read tales of far-off places, magic spells, and princes in disguise. She yearned for excitement in her life, and for someone with whom to share it.

That someone was definitely not the handsome Gaston, who had announced his intention to marry Belle because she was the most beautiful girl in the village. Belle considered Gaston self-centered and arrogant. Besides, she had other plans.

Belle's father, Maurice, was an inventor, although most of his inventions failed. "I'm about ready to give up on this hunk of junk," Maurice said one day, kicking his latest project.

"You always say that," Belle laughed. But I just know you'll win first prize at the fair."

With Belle's encouragement, Maurice finally finished one of his inventions. That afternoon, he packed it onto the wagon behind his horse, Phillipe, and headed for the fair.

Hours later, they were still on the road. "We'll have to take a short cut through the woods," Maurice decided.

The forest road was dark and scary. Then Phillipe heard wolves howling and reared up in alarm.

"Whoa, Phillipe, whoa!" Maurice cried. But the terrified horse bolted and threw his rider.

Maurice had to flee from the wolves on foot. Just when he felt his strength would give out, he stumbled through the rusty gates of a gloomy castle.

No one answered his knock, so Maurice stepped cautiously inside the door. "Hello?" he called.

"Shh! Not a word," a mantel clock whispered to a golden candelabrum.

"Oh, Cogsworth, have a heart," the candelabrum replied. Then he called out, "You are welcome here, monsieur."

Maurice was astonished to see a talking candelabrum. But when Lumiere invited him to warm himself by the fire, he sank gratefully into a giant chair.

By the time Mrs. Potts arrived with her son, Chip, to offer Maurice a nice cup of tea, he was quite enjoying himself. "What service!" he said.

Just then, however, the door burst open, and the Beast's shadow fell over the room. 'What are you doing here?" he growled.

The next thing Maurice knew, great claws had grabbed him and hauled him off to a barred cell in the dungeon.

Back in the village, Belle was waiting for her father to return when Gaston swaggered in with a proposal.

"Picture this," he said. "A hunting lodge, my latest kill roasting on the fire, and my little wife massaging my feet. And do you know who that little wife will be? You Belle!"

Belle couldn't think what to say. Finally, she replied, "I'm very sorry, Gaston, but I just don't deserve you." As she maneuvered to get away from him, Gaston fell out the doorway and into a mud puddle, right in front of all the villagers. "I'll have Belle as my wife," he fumed. "Make no mistake about that."

But Belle didn't hear him, for at that moment, Phillipe galloped into the yard.

"Where's Papa?" Belle cried. "You have to take me to him!"

The tired horse carried Belle back through the woods. When she saw her father's hat on the ground inside the gate, she knew she had to enter the forbidding castle.

Lumiere took one look at Belle, and realized she was the one they had all been waiting for, the one who would break the spell. So he led the girl to her father.

"Oh, Papa! We have to get you out of here!" Belle cried. But just then, the Beast entered.

"**P**lease let my father out. He's sick," Belle begged.

"He shouldn't have trespassed," the Beast replied, "There's nothing you can do. He's my prisoner."

"Take me, instead," Belle said.

"Then you must promise to stay here forever," the Beast replied.

So it was agreed. The Beast dragged Maurice out the door to an enchanted carriage and sent him home.

Belle was heartbroken as she watched her father leave. She had not even been allowed to say good-bye. But she knew she had to keep her promise to the Beast.

Then the Wardrobe in her bedroom told her that the Beast wasn't as bad as he appeared. And the food at the castle was delicious. So Belle tried to make the best of things.

Meanwhile, as soon as he returned to the village, Maurice burst into the tavern shouting, "Help! He's got Belle locked in a dungeon!" But when he spoke of "a horrible beast," the villagers decided the old inventor was crazy.

While the others laughed at Maurice, Gaston took his friend Lefou aside. "I have a plan," he said. He had thought of a way to try to convince Belle to marry him.

At the castle, Belle was not locked up at all. The Beast had given her permission to go anywhere in the castle she wanted...except the West Wing.

Soon, the West Wing was all Belle could think about. So when no one was looking, she crept in. She found a dirty room full of cracked mirrors and broken furniture. The only beautiful, living thing was the enchanted rose, glowing inside a bell jar.

She was about to touch it when the Beast roared at her. "Why did you come here?" he bellowed. "Get out!"

Belle was terrified. Lumiere and Cogsworth saw her as she ran through the halls, but they could not stop her.

She ran out the front door, saddled Phillipe and escaped into the freezing night.

As Belle and Phillipe raced through the woods, they glimpsed the wild yellow eyes of wolves in the darkness. But when they tried to run faster, Phillipe's reins caught on a tree branch. He reared up in fear, and Belle was thrown to the ground. Instantly, snarling wolves surrounded her.

Suddenly, the Beast's giant paw snatched one of the wolves and tossed him through the air. After a fierce battle, the wolves fled, whining into the forest. But the Beast had been hurt.

Belle was about to jump back on the horse when she noticed that the Beast had collapsed in pain. She hesitated only a moment before running to his side.

Belle helped the Beast back to the enchanted castle, and nursed his wounds until he was better. Before long, Belle and the Beast were reading books, eating meals, and taking walks together.

"Isn't it wonderful!" the enchanted objects agreed as they watched the couple becoming friends.

Finally, the Beast allowed the enchanted objects to dress him in new clothes.

"Tonight, when the moment is right, you must confess your love to her," Lumiere advised the Beast.

So that night, after dinner, the Beast led Belle into the ballroom and they danced together to a beautiful love song.

"Belle, are you happy here with me?" the Beast asked.

"Yes, but…" Belle said, "if only I could see my father, just for a moment."

"There is a way," the Beast told her. And then he brought out his enchanted mirror.

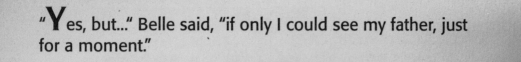

When Belle looked into the mirror, she saw her father lost and shivering in the woods, searching for her. "He's sick! He may be dying!" she said.

"Then you must go to him," the Beast said. "I release you. But take the mirror with you, so you will always have a way to look back...and remember me."

"How can you let her go?" Cogsworth asked, near tears.

"Because I love her," the Beast replied.

With the mirror's help, Belle found her father and took him home. "How did you escape from that horrible beast?" her father asked.

"I didn't escape, Papa. He let me go," Belle said. "He's changed somehow."

Meanwhile, Gaston had convinced the director of the insane asylum to lock up Maurice. His plan was simple. He would convince Belle that he was the only one who could save her father, but only if she agreed to marry him.

"Everyone knows her father is a lunatic, talking about some giant beast. But Belle will do anything to protect him," Gaston explained.

But when Gaston and the director arrived, followed by a crowd of curious villagers, Belle held up the enchanted mirror, and showed them the image of the Beast. "My father's not crazy!" she protested. "The Beast is real, but he's also kind."

Gaston realized that Belle had feelings for the Beast. Enraged, he snatched the mirror from her.

"She's as crazy as her old man!" he told the crowd. "The Beast will make off with your children. I say we kill him!"

And so the angry crowd followed Gaston through the woods to storm the Beast's castle.

The enchanted household objects saw the mob from the castle windows, and prepared their defense. By the time the villagers battered through the castle door, an army of angry objects was ready for them.

"Now!" Lumiere yelled, leading the attack. Immediately, forks and brooms and furniture and objects of every description hurled themselves through the air towards the astonished townspeople.

But the Beast, sure he had lost Belle forever, had no heart for fighting. "What shall we do, master?" Mrs. Potts asked him.

"It doesn't matter now. Let them come," the Beast replied. So when Gaston stormed into his room, the Beast didn't even attempt to defend himself.

When Belle arrived seconds later, she saw that Gaston had forced the Beast to the edge of the castle roof. "No!" Belle screamed.

The sound of Belle's voice snapped the Beast into action. He grabbed Gaston by the neck and dangled him over the edge of the roof.

"Let me go! I'll do anything!" Gaston pleaded.

Full of rage, the Beast hesitated for just a moment. Then he realized he was not really a beast at heart. He tossed Gaston safely back on to the balcony, and turned towards Belle, who had raced up the stairs to find him.

But just as the Beast moved to embrace Belle, Gaston pulled a long hunting knife from his boot...and stabbed the Beast in the back.

The Beast let out a howl of pain. Gaston took a frightened step backwards, tripped over the edge, and plunged from the roof.

But the Beast had been terribly wounded. Belle ran to his side and embraced him. "You came back," the Beast whispered. "At least I got to see you one last time."

"Don't talk like that. You'll be all right," Belle said, fighting back tears.

In the Beast's room, the last petal was about to drop from the rose.

"**N**o! Please don't leave me. I love you," Belle sobbed, leaning down to kiss him just as the last petal fell.

Magically, the Beast rose and changed back into his human form.

"Belle, it's me," said the Prince.

Belle rushed into the Prince's arms. As they kissed, magic filled the air. Soon Lumiere, Cogsworth, Mrs. Potts and Chip, and all the other enchanted objects were transformed back into their human forms.

That night, the castle was filled with love as Belle and the Prince danced and danced, barely able to take their eyes off each other. And the castle was once again filled with life.

Many strange legends are told of these jungles in India, but none so strange as the story of a small boy named Mowgli. It all began when the silence of the jungle was broken by an unfamiliar sound.

Bagheera the panther stopped to look around. He found a broken boat by the river and a basket containing…a Man-cub!

The baby smiled up at Bagheera. "It needs a mother," thought the panther. "The Man-village is too far away, but I know a wolf family with cubs." And so, he carried the basket to the wolf den.

The mother wolf came out and saw the Man-cub. How helpless he was! She carried him inside and snuggled him close to the other cubs.

And so Mowgli grew up with the wolf family, playing with his cub brothers and sisters, and loved by his wolf mother and his wolf father, Rama.

The wolf pack accepted Mowgli as one of their own, watching over him along with all the other cubs. Throughout the years, Bagheera often dropped by to see how the Man-cub was doing.

One night the wolves of the pack met at Council Rock. They had heard that Shere Khan, the great tiger, was in their part of the jungle. For many years he had been away, hunting cattle near the Man-village.

Shere Khan had learned of the Man-cub and had sworn to kill the youngster. You see, Shere Khan had grown to hate all men, for their fire and guns helped them best the tiger.

"**S**here Khan will surely kill the boy and all who try to protect him," warned Akela, the leader of the wolf pack. "The Man-cub can no longer stay with the pack."

"But," objected Rama. "He's like my own son. Surely he's entitled to the protection of the pack."

At that moment Bagheera came up to the Council Rock. "Perhaps I can be of help," he said. "I know a Man-village where he will be safe. Mowgli and I have taken many walks into the jungle together, so I'm sure he'll go with me."

"So be it," Akela replied. "Now there's no time to lose. Good luck."

The next day, Bagheera took Mowgli for a walk.

After a while Mowgli said, "Bagheera, I'm getting a little sleepy. Shouldn't we start back home?"

"Mowgli, this time we're not going back," Bagheera replied. "I'm taking you to a Man-village."

"But…why?" asked Mowgli.

"Because Shere Khan has returned to this part of the jungle. And he has sworn to kill you," Bagheera explained.

"But I don't wanna go back to the Man-village!" protested Mowgli.

As night was closing in, Bagheera was pushing Mowgli up a tall tree to sleep. "Go on. Up you go."

Mowgli grabbed hold of the panther's fur. Soon they were safe on a big branch. "Now get some sleep," yawned Bagheera.

Mowgli sighed and leaned against the tree trunk.

"S-s-say now, what have we here?" said a voice above his head. "It's a Man-cub!" A big greeny-brown snake slid down the trunk. It was Kaa, the python.

"S-s-sleep, little Man-cub," hissed Kaa, waving his head. Mowgli stared sleepily at the python. "S-s-sleep, s-s-sleep," whispered Kaa, winding his tail around Mowgli's body, tighter and tighter…

"Ah, Bagheera!" croaked Mowgli. The python hissed loudly.

"Kaa!" shouted Bagheera sitting up with a jerk. With one blow of his great paw he hit Kaa on the head.

The python's tail unwound and Kaa crashed to the ground. "Ohhh," he muttered as he slid away. "This is going to s-s-slow down my s-s-slithering."

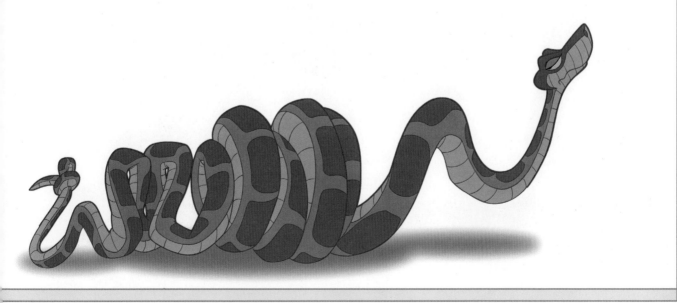

Mowgli and Bagheera were sound asleep the next morning when the jungle was shaken by the pounding of huge feet. "Hathi's Dawn Patrol," groaned the panther. Mowgli looked down and saw a line of elephants marching by.

"Hup, two, three, four!" bellowed the bull elephant in the lead.

"A parade!" cried Mowgli, swinging down from the tree on a long vine. He began to march at the end of the line, behind a baby elephant. "Hello. What are we doing?" Mowgli asked.

"Shhh! Drilling," said the baby elephant.

"Can I do it, too?" Mowgli asked.

"Sure," replied the baby elephant. "Just do what I do, but don't talk in the ranks. It's against regulations."

Mowgli began marching on all fours, but when Colonel Hathi ordered an about turn, Mowgli found himself nose-to-nose with the baby elephant.

"Company, halt!" cried Hathi. "Inspection!" He marched down the line. "Keep those heels together, shall we, son," he said to the little elephant. "Well, a new recruit, eh?" he asked, tapping Mowgli's nose. "I say, what happened to your trunk?"

"Hey, stop that!" cried Mowgli.

"Ha! A Man-cub!" roared Hathi. "I'll have no Man-cub in my jungle!"

By this time Bagheera had caught up with Mowgli. "The Man-cub is with me. I'm taking him back to the Man-village."

Hathi snorted. "Forward march," he cried to the elephants.

"Now, let's get out of here quick," said Bagheera, "before anything else happens."

"I'm staying right here," said Mowgli, sitting down in the middle of the jungle path.

After a tussle, Bagheera fell into the water. "That does it. I've had it, Man-cub!" scolded Bagheera. "From now on, you're on your own." And he walked off.

"Don't worry about me," said Mowgli. Then he sat alone in the jungle until Baloo, the happy-go-lucky bear, approached.

"Hey kid, you need help," said Baloo when Mowgli told him his story. "And ol' Baloo here's gonna learn you to fight like a bear." And so Baloo started to teach Mowgli everything he knew, including how to bend a tree to get the best bananas.

Baloo showed Mowgli how to fight and growl. When Bagheera heard the growling noise he ran back to see if Mowgli was in danger.

He was not very happy to find Baloo with Mowgli. Bagheera tried to explain to Baloo that Mowgli must return to the Man-village.

"Oh Baloo, I want to stay here with you," protested Mowgli.

"And just how do you think you'll survive?" asked Bagheera.

"I'll learn him all I know," promised Baloo.

"I give up," sighed Bagheera, walking away.

Soon Baloo was floating down the river with Mowgli on his tummy.

High above the river, several pairs of mischievous eyes watched the Man-cub. The orangutans swung down by their tails and grabbed Mowgli.

"Hey, let go of me!" yelled Mowgli. But it was too late.

The orangutans screeched as they leaped through the treetops. They raced on, tossing Mowgli back and forth and leaving Baloo far behind.

"Bagheera!" roared Baloo.

"What happened to Mowgli?" asked Bagheera, running over to Baloo.

"Them mangy monkeys carried him off," Baloo replied.

Immediately the two set off to find the boy.

Meanwhile, poor Mowgli was very dizzy when the orangutans finally dropped him beside King Louie's throne in the ruined city. "Word has grabbed my royal ear—have a banana—that you wanna stay in the jungle."

"Stay in the jungle? I sure do!" replied Mowgli.

King Louie would let Mowgli stay in the jungle if he told the king the secret of the red flower. "Have we got a deal?" he asked

"Yes sir! I'll do anything to stay in the jungle."

Of course, Mowgli didn't know the secret of the red flower, which was the jungle name for man's fire. Luckily, King Louie didn't bother to ask just then. He was so pleased with himself that he started to dance. The other orangutans and Mowgli joined in, singing and jiving in the ancient courtyard.

Baloo and Bagheera watched the dancing from the shadows. "Fire! So that's what that scoundrel's after," said Bagheera. "This will take brains, not brawn. Now, while you create a disturbance I'll rescue Mowgli. Got that?" asked Bagheera.

Soon a big new orangutan was dancing beside the king. It was Baloo, wearing a grass skirt and two pieces of coconut to hide his nose!

King Louie was delighted to see the big orangutan. The two of them jived and jumped together as they sang, paying no attention to anything. How long this would have gone on, nobody knows. But suddenly, what with all the shimmying and shaking, Baloo's disguise began to fall off. First the coconut halves, then the skirt…But he was enjoying himself so much that he didn't notice.

The king stopped smiling and shook his fist. The other orangutans stopped dancing, too. "It's Baloo, the bear!" they screeched.

"Yeah, that's him!" screeched another. "How'd he get in there?"

"Baloo, it's you!" gasped Mowgli.

Just as Baloo noticed that he was the only one still dancing, the orangutans grabbed Mowgli.

Bagheera leaped into the courtyard, but he couldn't get near the boy. The orangutans tossed Mowgli back and forth like a football, chattering and laughing the whole time. Baloo watched and waited, and when the orangutans threw Mowgli to the king, he grabbed one arm while the king grabbed the other.

"G-r-r-r!" roared Baloo, pulling as hard as he could.

King Louie pulled just as hard, hanging onto a pillar for support.

Mowgli was certain he was being pulled in half. Luckily, just at that moment the pillar collapsed and the old stone roof fell in, allowing Mowgli and his friends to escape.

"Man, that's what I call a swingin' party," said Baloo as they ran away.

Mowgli, Baloo, and Bagheera kept running, deep into the jungle. By the time they stopped, it was night. Mowgli nestled down on some grass and slept.

"Baloo," said Bagheera, "the Man-cub must go back to the Man-village. The jungle is not the place for him."

Baloo yawned. "Oh, stop worrying, Baggie."

"Sooner or later Mowgli will meet Shere Khan," warned Bagheera.

"Think what's best for Mowgli—and not yourself," Bagheera urged.

Baloo sadly shook Mowgli awake. "Mowgli? Mowgli—ah, it's time to get up."

After bidding goodbye to Bagheera, Mowgli and Baloo made their way through the jungle.

"Look, Mowgli," Baloo said at last, "I got to take you back to the Man-village."

"You're just like old Bagheera!" Mowgli cried as he ran off alone into the jungle.

Baloo could find no trace of Mowgli. Soon Bagheera joined him. When he found out what happened, the panther said, "Let's separate. We've got to find him."

Bagheera came upon the elephants. He asked Colonel Hathi for help in finding the Man-cub. The Colonel finally agreed.

Little did Bagheera know that Shere Khan was hiding in the tall grass, listening to every word. "How interesting," he muttered quietly to himself.

Not far away, Mowgli was walking through the jungle. Suddenly he was whisked up into a tree by Kaa.

But Mowgli managed to get away from Kaa and stomped off into the jungle.

On the edge of the jungle, four vultures sitting in a dead tree spotted Mowgli sitting alone, crying.

The vultures flapped their big, untidy wings and landed in front of Mowgli. "He's got legs like a stork, he has!" cackled one.

"Go ahead, laugh," said Mowgli. "I don't care."

"Poor little fella," said one vulture.

"Must be down on his luck," said another. "You know, you look like you haven't a friend in the world."

"I haven't," sighed Mowgli.

"Kid, we'd like to make you an honorary vulture," offered the vultures.

Shere Khan was creeping through the grass and heard the conversation. He lifted up his head and saw Mowgli with the vultures.

"Thank you for detaining my victim," the tiger said to the birds.

The vultures were as scared of Shere Khan as the other jungle animals. "Let's get out of here!" they squawked, flying up into the air with a loud flapping of wings. The storm that was brewing finally broke and the birds huddled on top of their tree. "Run, friend, run!" they shouted at Mowgli.

"Run? Why should I?" asked Mowgli, walking boldly up to Shere Khan.

"Why should you run?" growled the tiger. "Could it be possible that you don't know who I am?"

"You don't scare me. I won't run from anyone," said Mowgli.

"Ah, you have spirit for one so small, and that spirit is deserving of a sporting chance," Shere Khan replied. "Now I'm going to close my eyes and count to ten." When Shere Khan had finished counting, he leapt forward with a roar…and landed flat on the ground! Baloo had grabbed him by the tail!

"Let go, you big oaf!" growled Shere Khan. He knocked Baloo flat with one blow, and then ran after Mowgli.

Too late! The vultures had saved the Man-cub. But Baloo and Shere Khan continued to struggle.

Lightning flashed, setting fire to the vulture's tree. Mowgli quickly grabbed a burning branch and tied it to Shere Khan's tail. The one thing Shere Khan feared was fire, and he fled, howling with rage.

Mowgli hurried over to Baloo. "Baloo! Baloo, get up! Oh, please get up!" he pleaded.

Just then, Bagheera appeared. "You've got to be brave...like Baloo was," said Bagheera.

"You...you don't mean...oh, no!" cried Mowgli. "Baloo!"

Bagheera said, "It's best we leave now. Come along, Man-cub."

Baloo opened one eye. "Hey," he said.

"Baloo!" yelled Mowgli, giving him a big hug.

"Hey, Baggie," Baloo said to Bagheera. "Too bad you missed the action. You shoulda seen how I made a sucker out of 'Old Stripes' with that left up in his face."

The three friends were walking along a path in the jungle.

"Look! What's that?" asked Mowgli suddenly, pointing ahead.

"Oh, it's the Man-village," said Bagheera.

"Oh, no, I meant *that!*" said Mowgli, pointing to a pretty girl who had come down to a stream to fill her jug. "I've never seen one before." He moved closer.

"Mowgli, wait a minute!" called Baloo.

"Ah, Baloo, let him have a better look," said Bagheera.

Mowgli climbed onto a branch over the stream. The girl saw his reflection. She looked up and smiled.

Mowgli was so amazed that he fell into the water. The girl giggled and dropped her jug. Mowgli scrambled ashore, grabbed the jug, and followed her up the path. At the village gate he turned and gave his friends a goodbye grin.

Bagheera sighed happily. "Mowgli is where he belongs now."

It was a very important day in the Pride Lands. All the animals that lived there came from far and wide to celebrate the birth of King Mufasa's son. Rafiki, the wise old mystic, made a special mark on the new prince Simba's head. Mufasa and Queen Sarabi, Simba's mother, looked on with pride.

Then Rafiki held the cub high, at the edge of Pride Rock, so that all the animals gathered below could see their future king. The animals cheered for Simba, as he looked around bewildered. Then they all fell silent, and bowed to show their respect for him.

Mufasa's brother, Scar, was the only one missing from the ceremony. King Mufasa went to speak to his brother.

"Sarabi and I didn't see you at the presentation of Simba," said Mufasa when he reached Scar's cave.

"That was today?" Scar said in mock innocence. "Must have slipped my mind."

"Yes, well, as slippery as your mind is, as the king's brother, you should have been first in line," said Zazu, Mufasa's majordomo.

"I was first in line until that little hairball was born," replied Scar.

"That hairball is my son, and your future king," said Mufasa angrily.

Mufasa knew that Scar was smoldering with jealousy and anger because the young prince Simba had taken his place as next in line to be king. "What am I going to do with him?" worried Mufasa.

When Simba was a little older, Mufasa led him to the top of Pride Rock one morning at dawn.

"Everything the light touches is our kingdom," he explained. "One day, Simba, the sun will set on my time here and will rise with you as the new king!"

"What about that shadowy place?" asked Simba, looking into the distance.

"That's beyond our borders. You must never go there, Simba," Mufasa replied soberly.

"But I thought a king can do whatever he wants," Simba said.

"There's more to being king than getting your way all the time," his father replied.

Mufasa tried to explain to Simba what being king was all about. "Everything you see exists together in a delicate balance. As king, you need to understand that balance and respect all the creatures," Mufasa said. "We are all connected in the great circle of life."

But then news of invading hyenas arrived, and Mufasa had to leave Simba alone.

Later that day, Scar told Simba what that shadowy place was. "Only the bravest lions go there," he said slyly. "An elephant graveyard is no place for a young prince."

"Whoa!" Simba said.

Of course, the young lion couldn't resist proving how brave he was, so he ran to get his best friend, Nala.

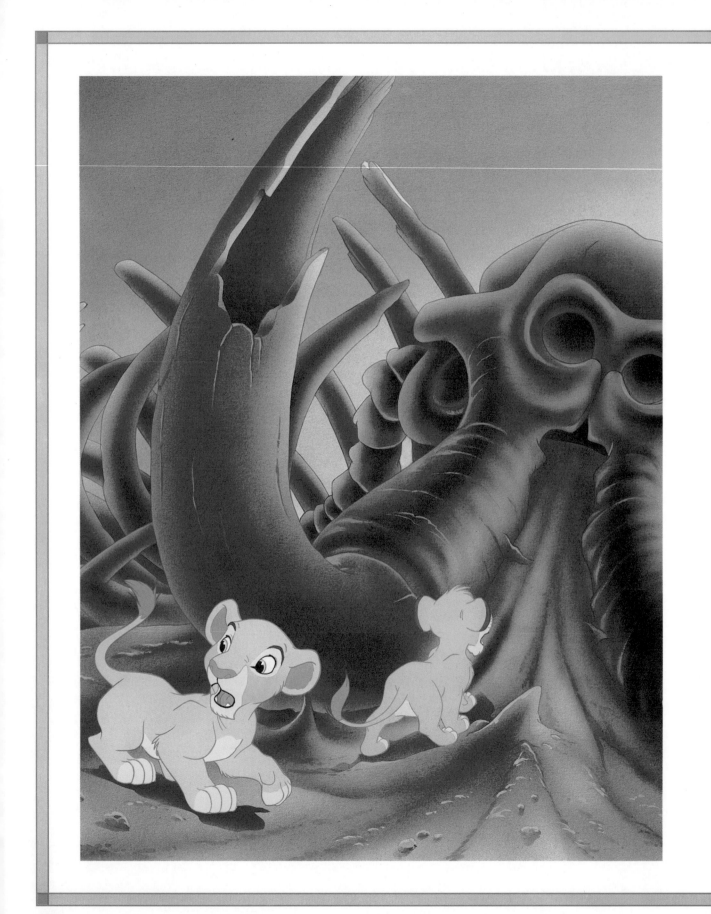

"**C**ome on!" said Simba. "I just heard about this great place!"

The two cubs soon escaped the watchful eyes of Zazu, who was supposed to baby-sit them. They headed for the shadowy place. Suddenly, they came upon an enormous, hollow-eyed skull. "This is it!" Simba announced.

"Whoa!" Nala said. "It's really creepy!"

"I know," Simba replied. "Let's go check it out!" He was about to climb into one of the huge eye sockets when Zazu caught up to them.

"We're way beyond the boundary of the Pride Lands," he said. "We are all in very real danger."

"I laugh in the face of danger!" exclaimed Simba. "Ha, ha!"

"Ha, ha!" answered the elephant skull. Suddenly, three hyenas appeared. They were not pleased that Simba and his friends had trespassed into their territory. They laughed their evil laugh before circling the threesome.

Zazu suggested that it was a good time to leave.

"What's the hurry?" Shenzi, one of the hyenas, said. "We'd love you to stick around for dinner."

"Yeah," Banzai added. "We could have whatever's 'lion' around, get it?"

The hyenas rolled on the ground with laughter—they loved a good pun. They kept coming up with new ones until they realized that their dinner was silently tiptoeing away.

The hyenas caught Zazu by the tail while the trio was making its escape. Simba returned to try to rescue the bird. He growled his most vicious growl at the hyenas.

"Why don't you pick on somebody your own size?" he shouted.

When Shenzi went after Nala, Simba scratched the hyena on the nose. The hyenas chased Simba and Nala into the rib cage of an old carcass, which snapped closed, trapping them inside like the bars of a jail.

As the hyenas crept towards the trapped lion cubs, they chuckled softly. Their long, sharp teeth gleamed in the dim light. Just when Simba and Nala were sure all hope was lost, a huge paw slammed at Shenzi, knocking her down and sending the other hyenas flying.

It was Mufasa, and he had arrived just in time. The hyenas were no match for him.

"If you ever come near my son again…" the Lion King roared.

The beaten hyenas fled with their tails between their legs.

"Zazu," Mufasa ordered, "take Nala home. I've got to teach my son a lesson."

When they were alone, he continued, "Simba, I'm very disappointed in you."

Simba tried to explain his behavior. "I was just trying to be brave like you."

"Simba, being brave doesn't mean you go looking for trouble," Mufasa said.

"But you're not scared of anything!" Simba insisted.

"I was today," his father said. "I thought I might lose you."

The Lion King and his prince looked up at the stars. "The great kings of the past look down on us from those stars," Mufasa said. "Those kings will always be there to guide you…and so will I."

Mufasa didn't realize that his own brother Scar was plotting to harm him and his son, in order to take the throne.

The next day, Scar led Simba into a steep gorge, telling him that Mufasa had a surprise for him. He left his nephew there, then signaled to the hyenas, who started a stampede of wildebeests through the gorge.

As Simba hung onto a tree for dear life, Scar yelled to Mufasa, "Quick! Stampede! In the gorge! Simba's down there!"

Mufasa leapt into the gorge and snatched the cub out of the path of the deadly hooves. He set Simba safely on a rocky ledge. But then the rock crumbled under Mufasa's paws, and he fell into the herd of wildebeests.

Mufasa was badly injured. Gathering all his strength, he tried to crawl back out of the gorge. Near the top, he saw Scar waiting for him on the ledge. "Brother, help me!" Mufasa begged.

Scar leaned down toward Mufasa. He pulled his brother close and whispered, "Long live the king!" Then Scar let go of Mufasa, and he fell into the stampeding herd.

The cub raced into the gorge, calling for his father. But when Simba finally reached Mufasa, the great Lion King was dead.

While Simba grieved, Scar suddenly appeared out of the dust. "Simba," he said, "what have you done?"

"He tried to save me," Simba answered. / "It was an accident. I didn't mean for it to…"

"The king is dead," Scar said. "If it weren't for you, he'd still be alive!"

"What am I gonna do?" Simba sobbed.

"Run away, Simba…run away and never return!" Scar told him.

Confused and heartbroken, Simba began to run. But he soon realized that the hyenas were following him. They chased the cub all the way to the edge of a plateau. There was only one way out. Simba leapt off the cliff into a tangle of thorns.

The hyenas were afraid of getting hurt in the thorns. Instead of following Simba, they shouted, "If you ever come back, we'll kill ya!"

With Mufasa and Simba gone, Scar was now the ruler of the Pride Lands. On his way to the top of Pride Rock to announce himself king, Scar made an announcement to the lions gathered below. "Mufasa's death is a terrible tragedy. But to lose Simba, who had barely begun to live... For me, it is a deep, personal loss."

Sarabi, Nala, and the other lionesses began to mourn.

"It is with a heavy heart," Scar continued, "that I assume the throne."

The wise Rafiki watched from a distance, shaking his head in disbelief.

Meanwhile, injured and exhausted, Simba stumbled across the hot African desert. Vultures circled above him. Finally, unable to go any further, he fainted. When he awoke, a meerkat and a warthog were standing over him. They had pulled him to an oasis and splashed water on him.

"You okay, kid?" asked the meerkat.

"You nearly died," said the warthog.

"Where ya from?" the meerkat asked.

"Who cares?" Simba said quietly. "I can't go back."

"Ah, you're an outcast!" cried the meerkat. "So are we!" Timon, the meerkat, and Pumbaa, the warthog, tried to encourage their new friend. "You gotta put your past behind you," they told Simba. *"Hakuna matata!"*

Simba followed Timon and Pumbaa to their jungle home. He soon adapted to their diet of bugs and grubs—as well as their easygoing lifestyle.

Time passed, and Simba grew into a young lion. He was happy, except when he thought about his father.

One day, he heard his friends cry out for help. He found Pumbaa stuck under a tree root, while a hungry lioness approached him. Simba quickly leapt into action and pounced on her. As the lions tussled, Timon gave Pumbaa a blow-by-blow account. "Get her! Bite her head! Go for the jugular!" Timon cried.

The lioness had Simba pinned to the ground when she suddenly paused. She and Simba looked into each other's eyes.

"Nala?" Simba asked incredulously. "It's me! Simba!"

Nala was delighted to find her childhood friend.

Simba introduced everyone, but Nala could not stop staring at him. "Everyone thinks you're dead," she said.

"They do?" Simba asked.

"Yes," she replied. "Scar told us about the stampede."

"What else did he tell you?" Simba asked warily.

"What else matters?" Nala cried. "You're alive! And that means you're the king!"

"King?" Timon and Pumbaa looked at each other in shock.

Simba and Nala went off into the forest to talk. Nala told Simba all about Scar. "Simba, he let the hyenas take over the Pride Lands," Nala said. "Everything's destroyed. There's no food, no water. If you don't do something soon, everyone will starve."

Simba hung his head and replied, "I can't go back."

Nala could not understand why Simba would not help the pride. "What's happened to you?" she asked. "You're not the Simba I remember."

"Listen!" he said angrily. "You think you can just show up and tell me how to live my life? You don't even know what I've been through."

That night, Simba was still thinking about his decision when an old baboon appeared. It was wise Rafiki! He told Simba that he could help him understand who he was and what he should do.

"I know your father," Rafiki said.

"I hate to tell you this, but he died a long time ago," Simba replied.

"Nope! Wrong again! He's alive," the baboon said. "I'll show him to you."
He led Simba to a pool of water and pointed to Simba's reflection.

A breeze rippled the water, and Simba saw his father's face.

"You see?" Rafiki asked. "He lives in you!"

Then Simba heard a familiar voice calling his name. He looked up at the stars and saw Mufasa's image.

"You are more than what you have become," Mufasa said, "You must take your place in the circle of life."

"How can I go back?" Simba replied. "I'm not who I used to be."

"Remember who you are....You are my son and the one true king...." Mufasa's answer echoed in the still night. "Remember...."

Then his father's image disappeared, and Simba was all alone.

Simba finally made up his mind to return home. As he crossed into his kingdom, he saw devastation everywhere. The great herds were gone. The grasslands were dead.

Nala, Timon, and Pumbaa soon caught up to Simba. When they saw some hyenas, Timon and Pumbaa distracted them while Simba and Nala headed for Pride Rock.

Meanwhile, at Pride Rock, the hyenas complained to Scar that the lionesses had not brought them any food for days.

"Scar, there is no food. The herds have moved on," Sarabi explained. Their only hope was to leave Pride Rock.

"We're not going anywhere," Scar growled.

"Then you have sentenced us to death," Sarabi replied.

"So be it," Scar said. "I am the king. I can do whatever I want!"

"If you were half the king Mufasa was..." Sarabi began. But the mere mention of Mufasa's name enraged Scar.

As Scar roared at Sarabi, he looked up and saw a great lion outlined against a blaze of lightning.

At first Scar thought that he was seeing Mufasa's ghost, but Sarabi recognized her son. "Simba!" she cried.

"Step down, Scar!" Simba said.

But Scar wasn't ready to give up. "If it weren't for you, Mufasa would still be alive! It's your fault he's dead!" Scar said slyly.

"Tell me it's not true!" cried Sarabi.

Scar and the hyenas quickly surrounded Simba. They forced him right off the edge of a cliff. Simba held on for dear life.

Scar looked down at Simba. "Now, this looks familiar," he sneered. "Where have I seen this before? Oh yes…This is just the way your father looked before he died….*I* killed Mufasa."

Now that Simba finally knew the truth about his father's death, his anger gave him strength, and he leapt toward his uncle.

Scar roared at the hyenas for help.

But Simba had friends, too. Nala and the other lionesses, as well as Timon and Pumbaa, attacked the hyenas. Scar took advantage of the confusion to sneak away.

He didn't get far, though, because Simba spotted his uncle at the edge of Pride Rock, and cornered him.

Scar begged for mercy. "It's the hyenas who are the real enemy," he said. "It was their fault—it was their idea!" Little did Scar know that the hyenas overheard his betrayal.

But Simba didn't believe his uncle. He repeated the advice Scar had given him years before. "Run away, Scar, and never return," he commanded.

Scar lunged at Simba. When Simba moved out of the way, Scar fell over the edge of the cliff. Simba could hear the sounds of hungry hyenas drifting up from the gorge, revealing his uncle's awful fate.

As rain began to fall, Simba stood at the edge of Pride Rock and roared triumphantly. The lionesses roared back with joy. The rest of the hyenas fled and were never seen again.

Soon, under the wise and brave Simba, the Pride Lands flourished. The herd returned to graze, the grasslands grew back, and food was plentiful again.

Not long afterwards, the animals gathered once more to celebrate the birth of the king's cub.

Simba and Nala watched proudly as Rafiki held their new cub high over Pride Rock.

Simba remembered his father telling him, "A king's time as ruler rises and falls like the sun. One day the sun will set on my time here and rise with you as the new ruler."

Simba would someday pass these same words on to his own cub, and the circle of life would continue.

Disney's THE ☙ LITTLE MERMAID

It was the day that all the undersea kingdom had been awaiting. Princess Ariel, the Little Mermaid, was going to make her singing debut. Her father, King Triton, was particularly proud. Ariel had the most beautiful voice in the undersea world, according to Sebastian, the crab. Sebastian was the castle's music director.

All the guests had assembled. Sebastian had tuned up the orchestra.

Ariel's older sisters began the concert, but when a giant seashell opened to reveal the Little Mermaid, Ariel was nowhere to be found.

"Ariel!" King Triton roared.

"My concert is ruined!" Sebastian wailed.

As usual, Ariel was off exploring with her friend Flounder. Ariel was fascinated with the world of humans. She loved collecting the strange objects they had dropped or lost in the sea.

Today, Ariel and Flounder were exploring a sunken ship, and found a fork.

She took it to Scuttle, the sea gull, to find out what it was. Scuttle considered himself an expert on humans.

"It's a dinglehopper," he declared. "Humans use these babies to straighten their hair."

Suddenly, Ariel remembered the concert. "Oh, my gosh!" she cried, and swam home as fast as she could.

Ariel didn't know that Ursula, the sea witch, was keeping an eye on all her activities. King Triton had banished Ursula from the palace long ago, and now she was plotting her revenge.

As Ariel had feared, her father was furious that she had missed the concert. "You are never to have anything to do with humans again. Never!" he commanded.

But then, after Ariel had left, King Triton felt some remorse.

"Maybe she needs someone to keep an eye on her," he sighed to Sebastian.

Sebastian soon found himself with a new job—looking after Ariel. He followed her to the grotto where she kept her treasures.

"If only I could be part of the human world," the mermaid said to Flounder.

Moments later, Ariel spotted a dark shape high above. "A ship!" she cried as she swam to the surface.

"No, Ariel!" called Sebastian. But Ariel did not look back.

Ariel had seen many ships before. But this was the first time she was able to swim close enough to see the humans onboard. They were having a birthday party for someone named Prince Eric.

When darkness came, the sailors lit up the sky with fireworks. But no one, except a big sheepdog named Max, noticed Ariel.

Prince Eric received a statue of himself as a
birthday gift from his friend Sir Grimsby.

"It's really something," he said in thanks,
though secretly he was embarrassed by the
huge replica of himself.

Then it was time for the humans to dance!
Even Max joined in!

The humans were having such a good time, and Ariel was so absorbed in the spectacle, that no one noticed the black clouds approaching.

In an instant, a great storm struck. Huge waves threatened to overturn the ship.

As lightning illuminated the sky, Ariel could see the sailors lower a lifeboat and scramble in. Eric noticed Max was missing and went back to search for him. Then, just as he lowered Max safely into the lifeboat, there was an explosion. Eric was tossed into the raging sea.

Ariel darted through the waves to the spot where she had seen the prince fall. Where was he? She plunged beneath the water and spotted him sinking fast.

Ariel managed to haul the prince to the surface, and hold his head above water until she pulled him ashore.

The next morning, Scuttle saw Ariel with the unconscious Eric on the beach.

"No pulse," he announced, listening to Eric's foot.

"No, look! He's breathing," Ariel said. "Oh, he's so beautiful!"

At that moment, she knew she loved Eric. She began to sing. Eric's eyelids fluttered.

Suddenly, Ariel heard Max bark. Ariel knew that Prince Eric's friends must be looking for him.

Ariel slipped quickly back into the sea, and hid behind a nearby rock so she could watch the beach. Sure enough, seconds later, Max sniffed out his master. He was followed by Grimsby who took the prince home.

All Eric could remember later was that someone had been with him. He had no idea what she looked like, but the sound of her voice lingered in his ears.

When Ariel got home, she was delighted to find the statue of Prince Eric in her grotto. Somehow, Flounder had been able to rescue it for her. "Oh thank you! I do so love him," Ariel sighed.

But when King Triton found out that Ariel had gone to the surface and met a human, he went straight to her grotto. "You disobeyed me!" he shouted. "If this is the only way to get through to you, then so be it!"

He raised his trident, and blasted Ariel's beloved treasures—including the statue, to bits.

Ursula watched the destruction from her palace and gloated with pleasure. "I think the time is ripe," she said to Flotsam and Jetsam, her slippery hench-eels.

Ariel was sobbing over the broken statue when Flotsam and Jetsam following Ursula's instructions, slithered up next to her. "We know someone who can help you," Flotsam hissed.

Ariel was desperate. She followed the pair to the sea witch's grisly den.

Ursula oozed sympathy. "The solution to your problem is simple, my dear," she purred. "You must become a human."

"But how?" Ariel asked.

"Just sign this contract," Ursula said. "It says that I agree to make you human for three days." In return, however, Ariel would have to surrender her beautiful voice to the sea witch.

And there was one other small clause—"If, after three days, Prince Eric does not kiss you, you belong to me!" Ursula said.

Sebastian who had followed Ariel to the rendezvous cried out, "No, Ariel! Don't sign! Don't listen to her!"

Ariel signed the contract, and Ursula worked her magic.

"Smart girl!" Ursula said.

Soon after, Ariel was above water on a beach, and Scuttle was staring at her new legs in wonder. "What's going on, Ariel?" Scuttle asked. There's something different about you."

"Ariel is not a mermaid anymore," Sebastian explained.

Prince Eric had been searching for the girl with the unforgettable voice. When he found Ariel, he hoped she was the one. But she could not speak, much less sing, so he decided she wasn't.

Still, this beautiful girl needed help. Eric invited her to be his guest.

At the castle, Ariel was given fine clothes
to wear and treated like an honored
guest.

And soon, just as she had hoped,
the prince seemed to be falling in
love with her.

On Ariel's second evening as a human, Eric took her for a romantic boat ride
in the moonlight. He was just about to kiss her, when Flotsam and Jetsam
overturned the boat, and ruined the mood.

"That was a close call!" Ursula exclaimed as she watched the scene in her
crystal ball.

She decided it was time for drastic action. So she disguised herself as a beautiful girl named Vanessa, and wore Ariel's voice in a locket around her neck. Then she made her appearance beneath the castle's walls, and let the voice work its magic.

When Eric heard her voice, he thought Vanessa must be the girl who had saved his life.

Eric made up his mind to marry Vanessa the very next day. The wedding would take place at sea, on his ship.

Vanessa was alone in her cabin before the ceremony, preening in the mirror, when Scuttle happened to look through the porthole. To Scuttle's surprise, he saw Vanessa's reflection in the mirror and realized she was really the sea witch!

"Soon I'll have that little mermaid, and her handsome prince, and the ocean will be mine!" he heard Ursula gloat.

"I've gotta tell Ariel!" Scuttle decided.

Scuttle found Ariel and Sebastian on shore, and passed along the horrible news. Then, while Ariel hurried to the ship, Scuttle organized a flock of birds and sea creatures.

Scuttle's army attacked Vanessa the moment she stepped onto the deck for the wedding ceremony. The locket broke from her neck, and Ariel's voice was released to its rightful owner, just as Ariel climbed aboard the ship.

"Oh, Eric..." Ariel said, finally able to speak again.

"It was you all the time!" Eric exclaimed.

But it was too late. "You belong to me, now," the sea witch screamed at Ariel, as she resumed her monstrous form.

The sun dipped swiftly below the horizon. The Little Mermaid's three days were up. The wedding guests stared in shock as Ariel became a mermaid again. In a moment, she and Ursula vanished beneath the waves.

Back under the sea, Ursula showed Triton his daughter and the signed contract.

"However, I'll give Ariel her freedom—in exchange for yours," she offered.

King Triton loved his little daughter so much that he agreed to the bargain.

"At last!" Ursula crowed. "I am sole ruler of all the ocean!" Then she used Triton's own magic trident to transform him into a pathetic sea creature.

Meanwhile, Prince Eric had gone in search of Ariel. "I lost her once. I'm not going to lose her again," he vowed.

Now, his harpoon flashed through the water, directed straight at the sea witch.

As soon as Ursula sighted the prince, she aimed the trident. But Ariel managed to throw Ursula off balance, so the deadly rays hit the sea witch's own evil eels instead of Eric.

Ursula was so enraged that her evil heart grew. And so did she, until she towered over the ocean.

"You pitiful fools!" she shrieked. "Now you will feel the power of the sea witch!"

Lightning flashed. Great waves swept over the sea, tossing up ancient shipwrecks from the seabed.

Eric managed to climb onto one of the wrecks. He steered it towards the mountainous form of the sea witch and impaled her on the ship's sharp bowsprit. With a bloodcurdling scream, Ursula disintegrated into a patch of bubbling black ooze.

With Ursula's destruction, Triton regained his power as king of the sea. At once, he went searching for his beloved daughter.

He found her on her favorite rock, staring longingly at Eric, who had been washed safely onto the beach.

And so King Triton granted Ariel her dearest wish. He made her human forever, so that she could marry Prince Eric.

The wedding was held aboard Eric's ship, with all the merpeople looking on from the sea.

Though King Triton was sad to know that his Little Mermaid would no longer live with him under the sea, his heart was happy knowing that she would always be with the man of her dreams.

Peter Pan chose to visit the Darling house because there were people there who believed in him.

Mrs. Darling believed Peter Pan was the spirit of youth. The boys, John and Michael, believed Peter Pan was a real person. They made him the hero of all their games. As for Wendy, their older sister, she was the supreme authority on Peter Pan. She knew everything about him. Even Nana, the nursemaid, believed in Peter, although being a dog, she kept her opinion of him to herself.

Mr. Darling was the only one who didn't believe. "Absolute poppycock!" he blurted when anyone mentioned Peter Pan. For Mr. Darling, the last straw came when he discovered the boys had drawn a pirate map on his last clean shirt front and hidden his cufflinks.

The boys explained that they had been playing Peter Pan and Captain Hook, and the cuff links were buried treasure. But Mr. Darling didn't want to hear a word about it. As far as he was concerned, it was all Wendy's fault. "Stuffing the boys with a lot of silly stories!" he said.

So he decreed that it was time Wendy had a room of her own. "I mean it, young lady. This is your last night in the nursery!" he ordered to everyone's dismay. And since he still had a full head of steam going, he fired the dog from her job as nursemaid, too, and tied her outside.

Wendy was troubled by her father's outburst, especially the part when he had told her she was going to have to grow up.

"But I don't want to grow up," she told her mother.
"Don't worry about it anymore tonight," her mother said.

John and Michael were upset too about Nana, Peter Pan, and losing Wendy from the nursery.

"Don't judge your father too harshly," Mrs. Darling told the children as she kissed them goodnight. "He really loves you very much."

Moments after Mr. and Mrs. Darling left for the theater, Peter Pan hopped through the nursery window. Right behind him was Tinker Bell.

They had come for Peter Pan's shadow. Peter had become separated from it on his last visit to the Darling house, and Nana had gotten hold of it.

"Must be here somewhere," Peter said, looking around the nursery. After some searching, he found it in the drawer where Wendy had put it after she'd found Nana chewing on it.

The shadow didn't want to be caught. It flew out of the drawer and made Peter chase it around the room, thumping into things.

The noise woke up Wendy. "I knew you'd come back!" she cried to Peter.

Wendy knew just what to do with the reluctant shadow, she'd sew it back on! So she got out her sewing kit.

Meanwhile, Peter explained how Nana had grabbed his shadow while he was lurking on the window ledge, listening to Wendy's stories.

"My stories? But they're all about you!" Wendy cried.

"Of course. That's why I like them," Peter said.

Wendy wasn't too happy to tell Peter the news that there would be no more stories. "I have to grow up tomorrow. Tonight's my last night in the nursery," she explained.

"I won't have it," Peter cried. "Come on. We're going to Never Land. You'll never grow up there!"

It took only a minute to wake John and Michael.

...**A**nd another few minutes for the Darling children to learn how to fly. It was quite easy to do, really, as long as you had a bit of Tinker Bell's pixie dust.

Then they were on their way to Never Land.

The island of Never Land is an extremely long distance from the city of London, or any other city for that matter. But because of the pixie dust, it was no time at all before the Darling children spotted it in the sea below.

"Oh Peter! It's just as I've always dreamed it would be!" Wendy cried.

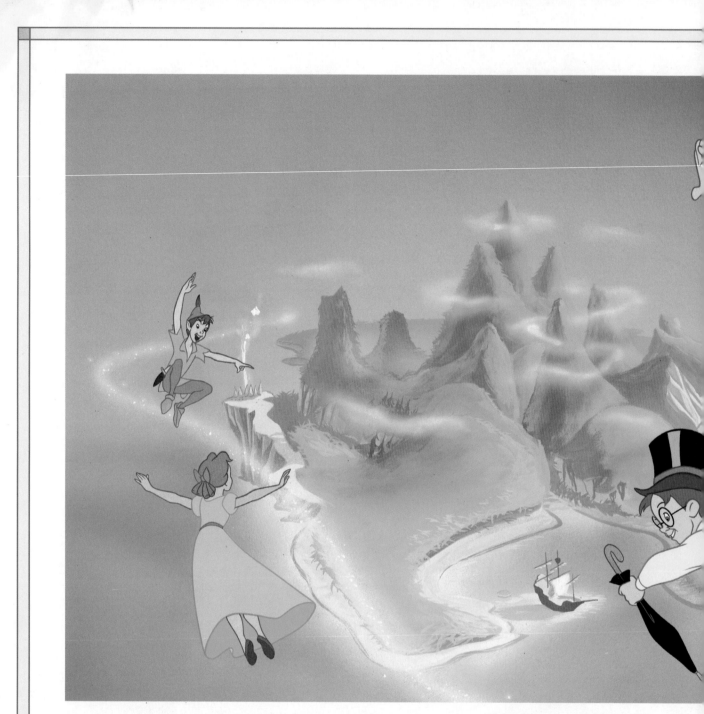

From Wendy's stories, the children already knew that Never Land was home to Peter and his Lost Boys, as well as an Indian tribe and a number of mermaids. They also knew that Peter's mortal enemy, Captain Hook, kept his pirate ship anchored in the harbor. And there it was, down below.

None of the Darling children was prepared for the welcome they received from the pirates. "Look out!" Peter cried as a cannonball came hurtling towards them from the ship's deck. Luckily the Darling children had already flown quickly out of the way.

"Quick, Tink! Take Wendy and the boys to the island," Peter shouted. "I'll stay here and draw Hook's fire."

Captain Hook and Peter had been enemies practically forever. As far as the pirate was concerned, Peter was the cause of all his misfortunes. He even blamed Peter for the fact that a crocodile followed him continually. The Crocodile had swallowed Hook's left hand a few years earlier and had been waiting for another taste of him ever since.

Fortunately, the Crocodile had also swallowed an alarm clock. The ticktock of the clock warned Hook whenever the Crocodile was around. Still, Hook was scared witless each time he saw it. He relied on Mr. Smee to keep the Crocodile as far from him as possible.

Hook had vowed to find Peter Pan's hide-out, so he could get even. He had sent his pirates to search Mermaid Lagoon, Cannibal Cove, and everywhere else.

By now the pirates were fed up. They wanted to get back to buccaneering. But Hook couldn't stop pouring over the map of Neverland, desperately searching for Peter Pan.

"I've got it!" he finally cried, pointing to the Indian encampment. "Tiger Lily! The Chief's daughter. She'll know where Pan is hiding!"

But before Hook could arrange to kidnap Tiger Lily, Peter and the Darling children flew into view, and Hook had ordered his pirates to fire the cannons at them.

Tinker Bell flew down towards Never Land, dodging cannon balls. Wendy and the boys followed far behind. "Wait! We can't keep up! "Wendy cried. But Tinker Bell thought Peter was paying far too much attention to Wendy. So she flew ahead and told the Lost Boys to shoot Wendy down.

Fortunately, Wendy was not hurt. But Peter was furious when he found out what had happened. "You blockheads," he said. "I bring you a mother to tell you stories, and you shoot her down."

Since Tinker Bell was behind the plot, he charged her with high treason and banished her for a week.

Later, John and Michael said they would like to see some Indians. "All right," Peter agreed. "John, you be the leader." So John led an expedition of Lost Boys through the jungle. Almost at once, they found some Indians. And the next thing they knew, they were tied to a totem pole.

John and Michael were worried, but the Lost Boys weren't. It was a game, they explained. "When we win, we turn them loose. When they win, they turn us loose."

But this time, the Chief wouldn't let them go. He thought the Lost Boys were the ones who had kidnapped Tiger Lily. And if she wasn't back by sunset, the boys would be burned at the stake.

Meanwhile, Peter had taken Wendy to meet some mermaids. But the mermaids ignored Wendy completely. Instead, they flirted with Peter and begged him to tell them one of his adventures. Peter started to recount the time he had been surrounded by fifty pirates when Wendy lost patience. "Oh, Peter!" she interrupted.

"Who's she?" one of the mermaids asked. "What's she doing here?" said another. "And in her nightdress, too!" a third remarked rudely, splashing water on Wendy's nightie.

Other mermaids tried to pull Wendy into the water. She was just about to smack one of them with a seashell when Peter stopped her. "They're just having a little fun. Weren't you, girls?" he said.

"That's all. We were only trying to drown her," one of the mermaids said.

"Well if you think for one minute..."Wendy started to say, but Peter put his hand over her mouth. He had just noticed Captain Hook and Smee rowing off in the distance towards Skull Rock...and they had Tiger Lily with them!

Quickly, Peter and Wendy flew off to get a closer look.

Captain Hook had a proposal for Tiger Lily whom he had tied in a place where she would soon be covered by the rising tide. "You tell me the hiding place of Peter Pan, and I shall set you free." Hook said. Tiger Lily was silent. "You'd better talk, my dear," Hook urged, "for soon the tide will be in, and then it will be too late."

"Stay here, Wendy, and watch the fun," Peter said, leaving her high on a cliff, out of danger. He flew behind a rock and lured Hook away from Tiger Lily by imitating the voice of a water spirit. "Beware, Captain Hook. Beware!" Peter intoned.

But Hook was not fooled for long. "Come down, boy, if you've a taste for cold steel!" he shouted. In response, Peter flew down to the Captain and did a little dance on the end of Hook's sword.

This was too much for Hook. He sprang into action. In the sword fight that followed, Peter managed to back Hook off the edge of a cliff.

The Crocodile was waiting below, its jaws gaping. Hook almost ran on top of the water in his effort to reach Smee and the boat!

Peter and Wendy rescued Tiger Lily and took her back to the Indian camp.

The chief released the Lost Boys and declared in sign language that Peter Pan was a mighty warrior for rescuing Tiger Lily. As a reward, he gave Peter an Indian headdress and a new title: Little Flying Eagle.

Afterwards, John was permitted to ask his fill of questions about Indian lore.

Meanwhile, Smee had managed to pry Hook loose from the jaws of the Crocodile and rowed him back to the ship with the Crocodile snapping behind them all the way.

The terrible ordeal had exhausted Hook. He was seriously considering giving up on getting even with Peter Pan. He would go back to his normal life, scuttling ships and cutting throats. But then Smee told him about the rumour that was going around:

Tinker Bell was jealous of Wendy. She had tried to kill Wendy, and Peter Pan had ended up banishing the little pixie!

"That's it, Smee! That's it!" Hook shouted. Quickly he dispatched Smee to find Tinker Bell.

Smee found her sitting dejectedly on a branch. He scooped her into his cap. "Begging your pardon, Miss Bell," he said, "but Captain Hook would like a word with you."

Hook was devious. He told Tinker Bell that he admitted defeat, and was leaving the island for good. He wanted Peter to know that he bore him no ill will, although he did think bringing Wendy to the island had been a mistake. "Rumour has it that already she has come between you and Peter," Hook said slyly.

Tinker Bell burst into tears, and Hook pretended to be sympathetic. Then, as if he had just thought of the idea, he offered a solution to her problem. "We'll shanghai Wendy!" he said. Now, if only he knew where Peter lived... .

Tinker Bell agreed to show Hook the location on the map if he promised not to lay a finger or a hook on Peter Pan. Captain Hook gave her his word, and Tinker Bell traced the path to Peter's hide-out on the map.

Hook thanked Tinker Bell, then trapped her inside a lantern!

Meanwhile, Wendy and the boys had returned to Peter's hide-out.

"Michael, take off that war paint and get ready for bed," Wendy said. "We're going home in the morning."

"Aw, Wendy, we don't want to go home." Michael whined.

"Let's stop pretending and be practical," Wendy said. "You need a mother. We all do."

But the boys seemed to have forgotten what a mother was. Wendy had to remind them. "A mother is the most wonderful person in the world..." she began.

By the time she had finished, John and Michael longed to go home. Even the Lost Boys, who had not seen their mothers in a very long time, felt sad and wanted to go home, too. So they all decided to leave Never Land that very night.

Peter was the only one who wanted to stay in Never Land. "Go back, and grow up!" he told the others. "But I'm warning you, once you're grown up, you can never come back."

As the boys marched out the door, Wendy stayed behind for a moment. She wanted to say good-bye to Peter. But he just turned his back on her.

As soon as Wendy stepped out of the tree, she saw that her brothers and the Lost Boys had been captured by pirates. She had no time to react and was carried away.

"And now, Smee, to take care of Master Peter Pan." Hook said as he placed a gift-wrapped box in front of Peter's door. Then he rang the bell.

But Hook had given his word to Tinker Bell not to lay a finger on Peter Pan. Or a hook, for that matter. "And Captain Hook never breaks a promise," he said.

Back on the ship, Captain Hook gave the boys a simple choice: They could sign on as members of the pirate gang, or they could walk the plank.

The boys were all about to sign when Wendy stopped them. "Peter Pan will save us!" she said.

"I don't believe you are in on our little joke." Hook said. "Sort of a surprise package, you might say." The package he had left at Peter's door contained a bomb, Hook explained. And it was set to go off within the next few seconds.

Tinker Bell overheard the conversation. She struggled desperately and finally overturned the lantern, shattering the glass. Quickly, she flew off to warn Peter.

Peter had found the package and read the note on it. "To Peter, with love from Wendy. Do not open 'til six o'clock."

The clock on the wall of his underground home said twelve seconds to six, but Peter couldn't wait any longer. He was untying the ribbon when Tinker Bell flew in. "Hi Tink. Look what Wendy left!" Peter said.

The pixie tugged at the package, trying to get it away from him. "Hey, stop that! What's the matter with you?" Peter cried.

Tinker Bell jingled furiously. "Hook? A bomb? Don't be ridiculous!" Peter said. Then he noticed the smoke coming out of the package... .

Kaboom! The force of the explosion rocked the ship in the harbor. Hook removed his hat and bowed his head for a moment. "So passeth a worthy opponent." he said. Then he turned to Wendy. "Which will it be, the pen or the plank?"

"We will never join your crew." Wendy replied.

"As you wish." said Hook. "Ladies first, my dear."

Wendy said, "Goodbye, boys." and she walked off the edge of the plank.

The pirates waited to hear the splash Wendy would make as she hit the water. It never came! A pirate looked over the side. "Not a blooming ripple!" he said. "It's a jinx, that's what it is!"

It wasn't a jinx; it was Peter Pan. He had arrived just in time to save Wendy. They listened to the pirates' conversation from their perch on the anchor chain. Then Peter flew Wendy to the safety of the crow's nest and turned towards the pirates. He had business to conclude with Captain Hook.

Meanwhile, Captain Hook was yelling at the pirates. "You want a splash?" he asked his worried shipmates. "I'll give you a splash! Who's next?"

"You're next, Hook!" Peter said. "Say your prayers."

Hook was furious that Peter had escaped the bomb. He lunged at Peter with his sword, but Peter darted and dodged so quickly that the Captain got his hook stuck in the mast. While he struggled free, Peter had time to untie all the boys. They joined the battle.

"Down, you blackguard!" John yelled, whacking a pirate with his umbrella.

Peter Pan and Hook fought along the mast. Every time Hook got close, Peter would fly away. "You wouldn't dare fight old Hook man to man!" The Captain taunted. "You'd fly away like a cowardly sparrow!"

Peter hated being called a coward. He gave his word he would fight without flying. "No, Peter. It's a trick!" Wendy shouted.

Peter ignored Wendy's warning and fought on. Hook backed him to the end of a yardarm, and Peter nearly fell off. Wendy couldn't stand to watch. She covered her eyes. Below, the Crocodile waited patiently.

Then Peter grabbed the skull and crossbones flag, and tangled Hook in it. Now the pirate was at his mercy. "Kill him!" the boys shouted.

Hook grovelled, "I'll go away forever! I'll do anything you say."

"All right," Peter said. "If you'll say you're a codfish."

"I'm a codfish." Hook said.

So Peter told Hook he was free to go. Then, as soon as Peter turned his back, Hook raised his arm to strike him with his hook. He missed, and lost his balance.

The Crocodile was ready for him.

"**H**ooray for Captain Pan!" the Lost Boys shouted.

Peter strutted across the deck like a captain. "All right, you swabs," he said. "We're casting off! Heave those halyards."

The boys scrambled back into the rigging.

"Peter," Wendy said. "Oh, that is, Captain Pan," she stuttered. "Could you tell me, sir, where we're sailing?"

"London, madam," Peter replied.

" John! We're going home!" Wendy cried joyfully.

While the Lost Boys raised the anchor, Peter called to Tinker Bell. "Pixie dust," he ordered.

Tinker Bell saluted and sprinkled pixie dust over the deck and rails. The pirate ship began to glow. Then it rose slowly from the water until Never Land was far below.

When Mr. and Mrs. Darling got home, they were puzzled to find Wendy asleep on the window seat.

"Oh, mother! We're back!" she said when they wakened her. "All except the Lost Boys. They weren't quite ready to grow up. That's why they went back to Never Land. But I am." she blurted out.

Her parents were completely confused.

"Ready to grow up," Wendy explained. She told them all about Tinker Bell, and the mermaids, and being saved by Peter Pan, and calling Captain Hook a codfish until Mr. Darling concluded that perhaps she wasn't ready to grow up after all.

"Perhaps we were a bit hasty," he said as he turned to leave the room. "I'm going to bed."

"He really is wonderful, isn't he?" Wendy said as she looked out the window. "See how well he sails the ship?"

Mrs. Darling glanced in the direction of Wendy's gaze. Then she called for her husband to take a look.

Mr. Darling stared at the ship for quite a long time. Finally, he said, "You know, I have the strangest feeling that I've seen that ship before, a long time ago, when I was very young."

"**W**here is Pocahontas?" asked Chief Powhatan. Everyone in the village had turned out to welcome home their leader and his brave warriors, everyone, that is, except Powhatan's beloved daughter, Pocahontas.

As usual, Pocahontas was off on an adventure with her two friends, Meeko the raccoon, and a hummingbird called Flit.

Her best friend, Nakoma, eventually found Pocahontas standing on her favorite cliff, lost in thought. "Your father's back!" Nakoma called.

Pocahontas headed home, excitedly. She was anxious to tell her father about the dream she kept having, a dream about a spinning arrow. She knew it meant something exciting was going to happen. But what?

Powhatan smiled when he heard his daughter's account of her dream and its meaning. "Something exciting *is* about to happen," he said. "Kocoum has asked to seek your hand in marriage." Then he gave his daughter a necklace. It was the same necklace her mother had worn at her wedding to Powhatan many years before.

Although Pocahontas was greatly moved by her father's gift, she did not want to marry Kocoum. He was certainly the bravest and most handsome of the young warriors. But he never smiled. And besides, she had a feeling her dream was pointing her down another path.

So she went to see Grandmother Willow for advice. "What is my path?" Pocahontas asked. "How am I ever going to find it?"

"All around you are spirits, child," the wise tree spirit said. "They live in the earth, the water, the sky. If you listen, they will guide you."

As if in response to Grandmother Willow's words, a breeze began to blow. Pocahontas ran to the shore and climbed a cliff, hoping to hear what the wind was telling her.

That's when she saw a sight she had never seen before. It was the *Susan Constant*, it's sails flapping in the breeze. The ship had sailed all the way from England, bringing settlers to the land where Pocahontas lived.

The first one off the ship was John Smith. Smith was anxious to explore this new land, especially after being cooped up on the ship for several months.

He had been given a special assignment by Governor Ratcliffe, the leader of the expedition. "I'm counting on you to make sure that any Indians we find won't get in our way," Ratcliffe had said.

"If they're anything like the ones I've seen before, it's nothing I can't handle," Smith had replied.

Now, onshore, Smith wandered quite close to the spot where Pocahontas had hidden herself. Meeko the raccoon couldn't resist the chance to investigate the stranger, and ran out to greet him. "You're a strange looking fellow," Smith said, holding out a biscuit.

Meeko was so excited with the gift, that he nearly gave away Pocahontas's hiding place. But just then, a bugle sounded, calling Smith back to the other settlers.

Smith had been summoned to watch Governor Ratcliffe plant the British flag. Ratcliffe said he was claiming the new land for his king and country. But all he really cared about was the gold and other riches he hoped to find.

Ratcliffe was ruthless and ambitious. He had promised the settlers freedom and prosperity in a new land. But he was willing to risk their lives for his own personal gain.

The only living thing Ratcliffe seemed to care about was his pug dog, Percy. Percy was so spoiled that he was carried around on a velvet cushion and fed better food than the settlers were given. Little Meeko soon made it his ambition to share Percy's luxuries.

After the flag-planting ceremony, Ratcliffe had the settlers begin to dig for gold.

Meanwhile, a party of warriors had spotted the settlers putting up their encampment near the shore. When they reported this to their chief, Powhatan asked Kekata, the village medicine man, to find out what the arrival of the white men might mean.

Kekata threw some powder on the fire. The smoke that rose from the flames took the shape of hungry wolves and of soldiers with weapons that spouted fire.

Powhatan realized the situation called for caution.

"Take some men to the river to observe these visitors," he ordered Kocoum. "Let us hope they do not intend to stay."

Meanwhile, John Smith was scouting in the forest, when he sensed he was not alone. Turning, he saw Pochahontas through the mist of a waterfall. They stared at each other for a long moment, before Pochahontas darted away.

"No, wait, please…" Smith called after her.

Then Pocahontas remembered what Grandmother Willow had said to listen with her heart to the voices around her. So she decided to stop and listen to this stranger.

As they got to know each other, Pocahontas realized that Smith had some odd ideas. For instance, he thought the Indians were savages. And he did not understand that all the parts of nature, people, animals, plants, even the wind and clouds, were alive and connected to each other.

So she showed John Smith her world. Slowly, he started to see the colors and shapes of the wind, and the rest of nature, just as she did. When they parted at the end of the day, neither one wanted to say good-bye.

Soon the tension between the settlers and Indians began to worsen. Ratcliffe had found no gold, and was furious. He was sure the Indians were hiding it all.

There had already been one confrontation near the settlers' encampment. One of the Indian warriors who had gone to observe the settlers with Kocoum had been shot and wounded.

"These white men are dangerous!" Powhatan said. He gave orders that no one was to go near the settlers again.

But Pocahontas ignored his order. She even ignored the warning of her best friend Nakoma, who told her to stay away from John Smith. Instead, when Smith came to meet her while she was out picking corn, she quickly left with him, leading him to Grandmother Willow's glade.

That's when she found out that the settlers had come for gold. "What is gold?" Pocahontas asked.

Once Smith had explained, Pocahontas told him that the only gold the Indians had was the golden corn they grew in their fields.

They were still talking when Grandmother Willow joined the conversation. "Hello, John Smith," she said.

Smith was shaken. "Pocahontas, that tree is talking to me," he blurted out.

"Don't be frightened," the tree spirit told him. "My bark is worse than my bite."

Soon, Grandmother Willow and John Smith were chatting away as if they had known each other for years. Pocahontas was pleased that Grandmother Willow approved of her new friend.

Suddenly, they were interrupted by the shouts of two settlers who were looking for Smith. Smith realized he had to get back to the settlement.

When Pocahontas reached home, she discovered that the Indians were preparing for battle. She went to her father and begged him to talk to the settlers, instead of fighting.

"It's not that simple," Powhatan replied. He was convinced that the settlers were not interested in talking.

When Smith returned to the settlement, he tried to explain to Governor Ratcliffe and the others that the Indians had no gold, only corn. He also explained that the corn was food, and that the Indians would be happy to share it.

But the Governor wasn't interested in even looking at the corn Smith had brought him.

Ratcliffe made his position absolutely clear. "Anyone who so much as looks at an Indian without killing him on sight will be tried for treason and hanged," he said.

Smith still believed that it might be possible to keep the peace with the Indians. So that night, he met secretly with Pocahontas at the enchanted glade.

Pocahontas suggested that Smith should come to her village and talk to her father. He was reluctant, until Grandmother Willow convinced him that someone had to take the first step towards peace.

"All right. Let's go talk to your father," Smith said. Pocahontas was overjoyed and threw her arms around him.

Just then, however, Kocoum stepped into the glade. Nakoma had sent Kocoum after Pocahontas, because she was worried for her friend's safety. When the young warrior saw Pocahontas in the arms of Smith, he attacked.

Smith's friend Thomas arrived just in time to see Kocoum with a knife raised against Smith. He fired his musket, and Kocoum fell to the ground...dead.

"Thomas, get out of here!" Smith yelled.

A party of warriors appeared moments later and dragged Smith away.

Powhatan condemned Smith to die at sunrise. And he had harsh words for Pocahontas. "Because of your foolishness, Kocoum is dead. You have shamed your father!" he said.

Meanwhile, Thomas carried the news of Smith's capture back to the settlement. Ratcliffe used the information to inspire the settlers to fight. This was what happened, he told them, when someone tried to befriend the Indians. He soon had them steamed up and ready for battle.

Meanwhile, Pocahontas had wandered back to the enchanted glade. She was heartbroken, but she could not think of any way to help Smith.

She was holding Smith's compass, which he had given to little Meeko. The compass arrow began spinning wildly, then suddenly stopped. It was pointing towards the sunrise...and John Smith.

Pocahontas realized it was the arrow from her dream. She began to run in the direction the arrow was pointing.

Just before sunrise, the Indians arrived at the place of execution. The settlers were also marching, armed and angry, to the same spot. It seemed that nothing could prevent bloodshed now.

Then, just as Powhatan raised a huge club over Smith, Pocahontas appeared.

She threw herself over Smith and shouted, "No! If you kill him, you'll have to kill me, too! Look around you. This is where the path of hatred has brought us."

No one moved. Then Pocahontas said, "You have the power to change that, Father."

Powhatan heard the wisdom of his daughter's words. "From this day forward there will be no more killing," he announced. "Let us be guided instead to a place of peace."

When the Indian warriors put down their weapons, Ratcliffe yelled, "Now's our chance, men. Fire!"

But the settlers had finally understood how greedy Ratcliffe was. They lowered their weapons, too.

In desperation, Ratcliffe reached for a gun and fired at Powhatan. John Smith hurled himself in front of the chief and was shot instead.

The settlers were enraged. They grabbed Ratcliffe, put him in chains, and dragged him to the ship.

The next day, the settlers readied the *Susan Constant* to set sail for England. The Indians brought blankets and food for their journey.

John Smith lay on a stretcher, ready to be carried onboard. Thomas told Pocahontas that Smith would die if he stayed behind.

"Going back is his only chance," Thomas explained. Powhatan placed his own cloak over Smith. "You are always welcome among our people," he said. "Thank you, my brother."

Then Pocahontas approached Smith. She had brought a small pouch for him. "It's from Grandmother Willow's bark," she said. "It will help with the pain."

Come with me," John Smith begged.

Pocahontas looked to her father for advice. "You must choose your own path," Powhatan said.

Then Pocahontas looked at the Indians sharing food with the settlers. It was the first sign of peace, and she had made it happen.

Suddenly, Pocahontas realized what her dream had meant, and what her path must be. She would continue working for peace between her people and the newcomers.

As Pocahontas watched the Susan Constant sail away, a gentle wind whispered in her ear. She knew that the same wind would carry John Smith safely -home.

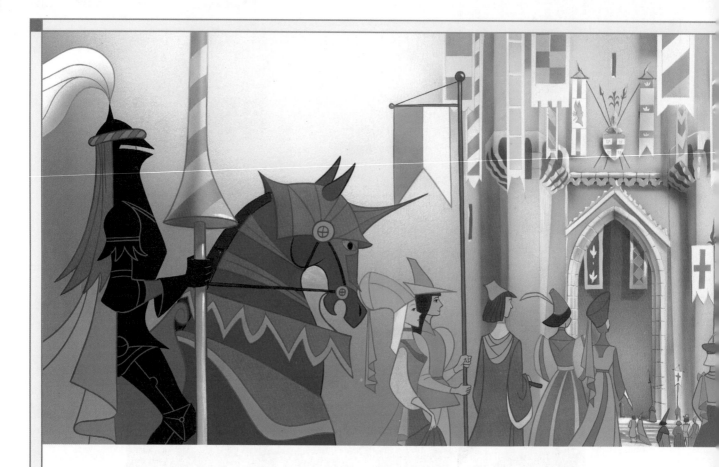

Long ago, in a faraway land, there lived a king named Stefan and his lovely Queen. They longed for a child, but for many years their wish was denied.

Then, one happy day, their wish came true. A golden-haired baby girl was born. They called her Aurora in honor of the dawn, for she had brought sunshine into their lives.

King Stefan and the Queen were so delighted that they declared a holiday in all the kingdom. A great festival was planned, and everyone was invited to the castle to celebrate the birth of the little princess. The royal cradle was brought into the great throne room for all to see.

The visitors from far and near brought gifts and good wishes and pledged their loyalty to the new princess. From the neighboring kingdom came King Hubert and his young son Phillip.

The two kings were old friends. They thought it would be a fine thing if Phillip and Aurora would marry one day when they grew up. This is how Aurora became betrothed to the prince while she was still in her cradle.

The Queen showed Phillip the pretty baby in its royal crib, but Phillip wasn't very interested in babies and couldn't imagine himself marrying one!

Last to bring their gifts were the three good fairies. Flora, followed by Fauna and Merryweather. They flew slowly down from the top of the great hall, sunshine twinkling all around them, and gathered around the royal crib. "The little darling!" sighed Merryweather.

"Your majesties," said Flora, "each of us may bless the child with a single gift, no more, no less. Little Princess, my gift shall be the gift of beauty." She waved her magic wand, and a sprinkle of stardust settled on the crib.

Fauna was next. "My gift shall be the gift of song." She waved her wand, and the sound of sweet birds singing surrounded the baby.

Merryweather was about to give her gift when a fierce wind blew open the great hall door.

The wicked Maleficent appeared, furious at not having received an invitation!

"To show I bear no ill will, I too shall bestow a gift on the child. Listen well all of you: The princess shall indeed grow in grace and beauty, beloved by all who know her."

"**B**ut before the sun sets on her sixteenth birthday, she shall prick her finger on the spindle of a spinning wheel and die."

With a burst of evil laughter, Maleficent disappeared in a flash of lightning. The terrified Queen hugged her baby tightly as the three good fairies hurried up to the royal couple.

"Don't despair, your majesties," said Flora. "Merryweather still has her gift to give."

"She can undo this fearful curse?" asked the king.

"Oh, no, sire," said Merryweather.

"Maleficent's powers are far too great," added Flora.

"But she can help," said Faura.

Merryweather nodded eagerly, and waved her wand. "Sweet princess, if a spindle should your finger prick, a ray of hope there still may be in this the gift I give to thee. Not in death, but just in sleep, the fateful prophecy you'll keep. From this slumber you shall wake, when true love's kiss the spell shall break."

To be safe, the king ordered that all the spinning wheels and spindles in the land be burned. That night, there was a huge bonfire in the courtyard.

The good fairies had a better plan. "A bonfire won't stop Maleficent," said Merryweather.

"But there must be some way," said Flora.

They decided to disguise themselves as peasant women and to raise the baby in an abandoned cottage deep in the forest. If they did not use their magic, Maleficent would never guess where they were. Once Aurora was sixteen, they would return her to the castle.

And with a final wave of her wand, she turned their fairy robes into peasant dresses. Fauna and Merryweather were delighted.

Of course, the fairies had to convince the King and Queen of their plan. It wasn't easy. It would mean that the royal couple would not see their only child for sixteen years. And could they be sure that Maleficent wouldn't find out?

The fairies explained that it was the only way to escape the curse. The king and Queen felt they would do anything for their little daughter, and at last, with heavy hearts, they agreed.

They watched from a balcony as the three fairies hurried away in the moonlight, carrying the precious baby.

Deep in the forest, the good fairies raised Aurora, calling her Briar Rose. As far as she knew, she was just a simple peasant girl. She was sweet and helpful, but a bit lonely because she knew no other children.

Nearly sixteen years passed. In her castle atop the Forbidden Mountain, Maleficent became impatient. She knew the princess was not in the king's castle.

"She couldn't have vanished into thin air!" raged the wicked fairy.

She called for her raven. "My pet," she said, stroking the bird's black feathers, "you are my last hope. Search for a maid of sixteen with hair of sunshine gold and lips red as the rose. Go, and do not fail me!"

With a croak, the evil bird flew off into the night.

The good fairies watched carefully over the princess. Each year she had become more beautiful, although she was still lonely. She would often daydream about the future.

On the morning of her sixteenth birthday, Briar Rose opened the shutters and shook out her dusting rag, humming to herself. She felt sure that it would be a happy day.

The fairies planned to make a beautiful dress for the princess as a special surprise for her birthday celebration in the castle. Of course, Briar Rose knew nothing about this.

"We want you to pick some berries," they said to Briar Rose, to get her out of the way.

Briar Rose had picked berries only the day before, but she agreed to go, out of love for the women who had raised her.

"Don't speak to strangers!" the fairies called as they shushed her out the door.

Briar Rose wandered through the woods singing to the birds, who twittered and fluttered about her as she walked. From a small hill, she gazed wistfully at the distant castle.

Someone else was in the woods that day. It was Phillip, the young Prince, riding to King Stefan's castle for the Princess's birthday celebration.

"You hear that, Samson?" Phillip asked his horse. They both stopped to listen. "Beautiful. What is it? Let's find out. There was something strange about that voice, too beautiful to be real."

Faithful Samson galloped in the direction of the singing.

As Phillip came closer to the singing, he hid behind some reeds beside a pond. Just at that moment, Briar Rose sat down on the opposite bank.

"Why do they still treat me like a child? They never want me to meet anyone," she sighed to the birds.

But you know something?" she added. "I have met someone."
"Who? Who?" asked the owls.

"Oh, a prince," she answered. "We walk together and talk together, and just before we say goodbye he takes me in his arms and then...I wake up. Yes, it's only in my dreams. But they say if you dream a thing more than once, it's sure to come true, and I've seen him so many times!"

Briar Rose got up and began to dance, singing about her dream prince. As she slowly twirled, she heard a voice singing along with her and felt two strong hands clasp hers.

"Oh!" she cried, turning around in surprise.

"I'm awfully sorry," said Phillip. "I didn't mean to frighten you."

It wasn't that. It's just that you're a..."

"A stranger? But don't you remember, we've met before, you said so yourself."

Briar Rose was rather timid. She had never met someone young like herself, and she also remembered the fairies' warning. But before long she was dancing with the prince, exactly as if they were in a ballroom.

"Who are you? What's your name?" he asked gently.

"My name? Why it's...Oh no, I can't! Goodbye!" She slipped from his arms and started to run.

"But when will I see you again?" he called.

"Never! Well, maybe someday...this
evening, at the cottage in the glen!"
And with that she hurried away.

Back in the cottage, the three fairies were very busy. Flora was trying to make a dress for Briar Rose, measuring it on Merryweather. Fauna was trying to bake a birthday cake. The dress was a disaster, and the cake melted into a gooey mess.

"Enough of this nonsense!" shouted Merryweather, stamping her foot.

"I'm going to get those wands." The sixteen years were almost up, and she wanted to make this birthday really special!

But Flora and Fauna worried that if they used their magic, Maleficent would find them.

There didn't seem to be any other way. The fairies closed all the doors and shutters, and set to work.

Flora produced a lovely gown with a wave of her wand. Fauna flicked her wand too, and soon flour, eggs, and milk mixed themselves into delicious cake. Merryweather twirled her wand and ordered the brooms to clean the room.

But then Flora and Merryweather got into an argument about the color of Briar Rose's dress.

"Pink!" said Flora.

"Make it blue!" cried Merryweather with a wave of her wand.

Soon pink and blue magic was shooting up the chimney, the one opening the fairies had forgotten to block!

High above the forest, Maleficent's pet raven was searching for a golden-haired maiden with lips red as the rose. When he saw the pink and blue magic light streaming up from the cottage chimney, he flew down to have a closer look.

Just at that moment, Briar Rose arrived at the cottage door. "Where is everybody?" she called, pushing open the door. There, beside the fireplace, was the most beautiful dress she had ever seen.

"Surprise, surprise! Happy birthday!" cried the three fairies, popping out from behind the door.

But Briar Rose couldn't wait to tell the fairies about the young man she had met. "Everything's so wonderful. He's coming here tonight."

"This is terrible!" cried the fairies. "You must never see that young man again."

"Why?" asked Briar Rose.

'You're already betrothed," said Fauna

"Since the day you were born," added Merryweather.

"To Prince Phillip," finished Fauna.

"But that's impossible! I'd have to be a..."

"A princess!" cried the fairies.

"And you are, dear. Princess Aurora. Tonight we're taking you back to your father, King Stefan."

That was all the raven needed to hear. With a gleeful croak, he flew off to tell his evil mistress the good news.

It was a sad Princess Aurora who set out with the three fairies for the castle that evening.

In the castle all was ready for Princess Aurora's return. King Stefan and his old friend, King Hubert, had already begun to celebrate.

"To the future," cried King Hubert, raising his wine goblet. Just then, Phillip came galloping into the castle courtyard. King Hubert hurried out to meet him.

"Change into something suitable!" cried Hubert. "You can't meet your future bride looking like that."

"But I have met her, Father," Phillip replied.

"What?" shouted the king. "NO, Phillip! Stop! Come back!"

But Phillip was already riding away.

Maleficent lost no time in flying to the castle. She watched as the fairies left Aurora alone in a room.

No sooner had they gone than a glowing green light appeared in the room. Like a sleepwalker, Aurora followed the light up a curving flight of stairs. At the top, she entered a small chamber. In the middle of it stood a spinning wheel and a spindle with a sharp needle.

An evil voice spoke. "Touch the spindle. Touch it, I say!"

Aurora reached out her hand and touched the needle on the spindle. As she fell to the ground, the three fairies rushed through the door.

"Ha! You poor simple fools, thinking you could defeat me. Well, here's your precious princess!" cried Maleficent, pointing to the seemingly lifeless Aurora.

The good fairies were miserable. "Poor King Stefan and the Queen. They'll be heartbroken," said Merriweather.

"We'll put them all to sleep until Rose awakens!" said Flora.

To Aurora they said, "You'll awaken to love's first kiss."

The fairies flew about, putting everyone from the king to the cook to sleep. But as Flora flew by King Hubert, she heard him mutter that Prince Phillip had fallen in love with a peasent girl that very day.

"Rose! Prince Phillip! Oh! Oh! Come!' she gasped. "We've got to get back to the cottage!"

Maleficent's raven had heard Briar Rose say her young man was to visit the cottage that evening. When Phillip reached the cottage, he knocked at the door.

"Come in," said Maleficent sweetly.

The moment Phillip stepped inside, he was attacked by dwarf-like monsters. Maleficent's goons! They carried him off to Maleficent's dungeon.

The three fairies arrived to find Phillip's hat on the floor. "Maleficent!" they gasped. "The Forbidden Mountains!" The fairies knew that they must free the princess's first love if Merryweather's prophecy was to come true.

They found the prince in the dungeon and gave him a magic Shield of Virtue and a Sword of Truth to protect himself.

The fairies told Phillip that Briar Rose was really Princess Aurora. They explained that she was asleep in King Stefan's castle, waiting for love's first kiss to awaken her.

Armed with his magic shield and sword, the prince escaped from Maleficent's castle. Outside, his faithful horse Samson waited for him.

Maleficent soon learned that Phillip was free. Her goons fired arrows at him as he galloped away, but the good fairies turned the arrows into flowers.

The enraged Maleficent saw it all. "A forest of thorns shall be his tomb!" she cried. She whirled her magic staff above her head, and at that moment a thick forest of thorny vines sprang up around King Stefan's castle.

Phillip galloped up to the thorns and began hacking at them with his enchanted sword. With a little help from the fairies, he chopped his way through to the castle drawbridge, where it crossed a deep canyon.

Maleficent saw the prince cut through the thorns. She flew to the drawbridge.

"Now you shall deal with me!" she shrieked.

Lightning flashed, and there stood a dragon, shooting flames.

Phillip held up his magic shield for protection, then threw his magic sword like a spear, piercing the evil fairy's heart. With a dying scream, she fell into the canyon below.

The prince hurried into the castle, past the sleeping soldiers and guests, and up the winding staircase to the top of the tower. There, on a bed covered with silks and velvet, lay Princess Aurora in a deep sleep. She clasped a single rose.

Phillip recognized his lovely peasant girl of the forest right away. He walked softly up to the bed, and kneeled beside it to kiss the princess.

Aurora's eyelids fluttered. She looked up at the prince. It was her dream come true!

At the very same moment of the prince's kiss, everyone in the castle began to wake up, though they didn't realize that they had even been sleeping.

In the throne room King Stefan yawned, then nudged King Hubert who was sitting beside him.

"Now, ah, you, ah, were saying...?" asked King Stefan.

"Oh yes!" said the sleepy Hubert, yawning too. "Well, to come right to the point, my son Phillip says he's going to marry..."

But King Hubert didn't have a chance to finish. Just then, the court trumpeters began to play a loud fanfare. The two kings looked up at the great staircase.   What they saw made them rub their eyes in amazement.

There, walking down the stairs arm-in-arm, were Prince Phillip and Princess Aurora. They were smiling lovingly at each other.

"It's Aurora!" cried the delighted King Stefan.

"And Phillip!" shouted King Hubert.

The king and Queen hugged their daughter, hardly believing their joy. Hubert nudged Phillip. "What does this mean?" But before Phillip could speak, Aurora kissed the king on the forehead. That was as good an answer as any!

Phillip took Aurora in his arms. The good fairies watched as the young couple waltzed around the throne room.

Fauna sighed, "Oh, I just love happy endings."